# Postman Pat's
## White Christmas

*Story by* John Cunliffe    *Pictures by* Jane and Joan Hickson
*From the original Television designs by Ivor Wood*

It began to snow on Monday.

Mrs Goggins said, "Lovely, we'll have a white Christmas."

There was more snow on Tuesday.

Katy and Tom said, "Great! We'll make a snowman!"

There was still more snow on Wednesday.

Pat said, "That's enough of this snow. It's getting tricky on the roads."

It came down like feathers on Thursday.

Miss Hubbard said, "We don't want any more of this snow. We'll be getting blocked in for Christmas."

It snowed all night, and the wind got up.

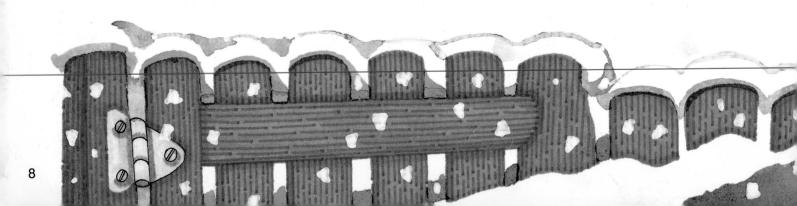

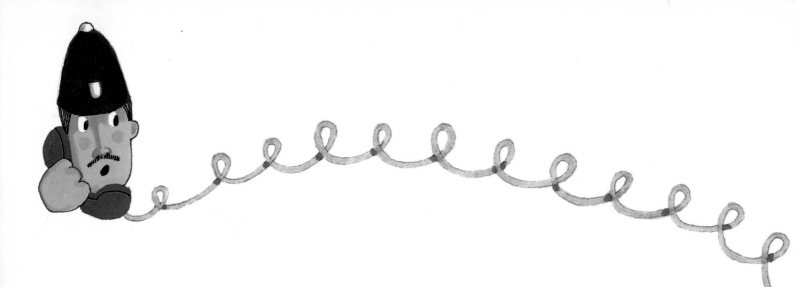

On Friday, PC Selby rang Pat first thing in the morning.  He said, "You might as well stay in bed.  There won't be any post today.  There are huge snowdrifts blocking the Pencaster Road, and the snow-plough's broken down.  We look like being cut off for Christmas."

"No Christmas post?" said Pat.  "That won't do."

Pat put his wellingtons on, and climbed up a snowdrift.  He sank in up to his middle and got stuck.

"That won't do," said Pat.

Ted came and dug him out.

"Let's dig through it," said Pat.

The snow fell in and filled the hole,
when they went for their lunch.

"That won't do," said Pat.

Peter Fogg said, "Let's try the big tractor."

Its wheels began to spin on the ice.
It was stuck.

"That won't do," said Pat.

"Have a look in my attic," said Granny Dryden.

"What are these?" said Pat.

"Skis," said Granny Dryden. "My old dad used them, once."

"*They* might do," said Pat.

Pat tried the skis.  He fell over and sat down in the snow.

23

He tried again.  He went a little way.

"I'm getting the idea," said Pat.

He practised all morning.

"It makes a change," said Pat.

"Let's try again."

He whizzed over a snowdrift.

"That's better," said Pat, "and it's fun!"

Then he skied all over Greendale to deliver it.

"That'll do nicely," said Pat.

And everyone was delighted to get their Christmas cards on time, no matter how deep the snow was.